Remmy The Reinicorn Saves Christmas

by Bryan Crown

illustrated by Daniel Howard

Hey Y'all! I'm Jippers the elf,
and the narrator of this story.
This book should be called,
"Jippers saves Christmas in all its glory."

I'll tell you why I was the one
to save Christmas and all the fun.

Find a spot, no need to push,
as I tell you a story of an amazing tush.

Christmas morning last year

Twas the morning of Christmas
and all through the house,
all the creatures were stirring,
even a small louse.

Kids woke up their parents as they knew they ought.
Screaming, "Let's go see what Santa Claus brought!"

Grumblin and mumblin they got out of bed,
and went with their children to see the great spread.

As they reached the room
where the presents should be,
they saw Santa munching on half a cookie.

"Poor Dasher, Dancer, Prancer, and the rest,
have sadly not been able to be at their best.

They are old, very tired, and oh so worn out,
which is making me frustrated and wanting to pout."

"With ten thousand more houses where we need to be,
I'm needing some reindeer with a little more spree.

I don't want to lose all the reindeer I've got,
but I need something special to prevent being caught."

"Sorry for rambling."
as he left with no warning.

"Merry Christmas to all
and to all a good... morning?!"

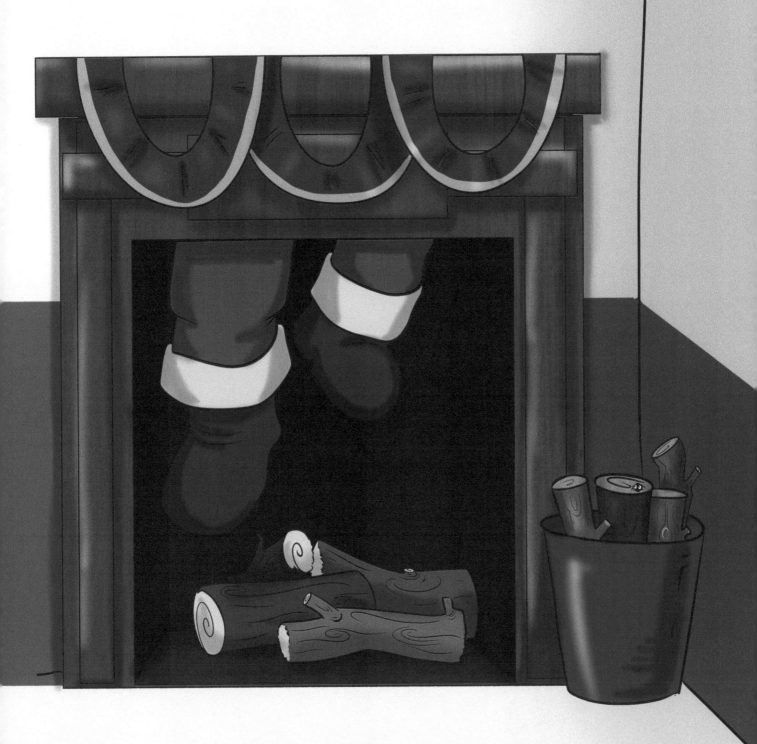

Just look at this light,
and dream of the night.

Hey! Y'all okay?
Those elves just erased your memo-ray.

I really get tired of having to rhyme,
but we elves must do it all the time.

Since your brains have recently been erased,
let me just cut right to the chase...d

Of how I, Jippers, solved Santa's problem,
let me finish the story of a really cool bottom.

Drum roll please!
Here's the king who cuts the cheese!

Badadadadadadadada....

Ta-da!

Remmy!

He's a reinicorn
who toots his horn.

He's the son of Comet and Veronica.
A unicorn who plays the harmonica.

They were sadly shunned for their strange marriage,
and couldn't show off what was in their carriage.

Why couldn't Comet just
marry a nice reindeer?

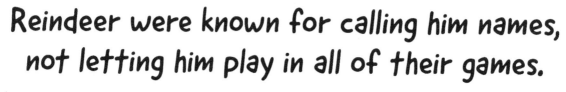

Reindeer were known for calling him names,
not letting him play in all of their games.

So Remmy grew up without a good friend,
but let me tell you about his rear end.

pfft

Remmy's round rump really tends to jump,
and when he eats dairy the explosions are scary.
He loves ice cream much more than pie,
but it makes him rocket across the sky!

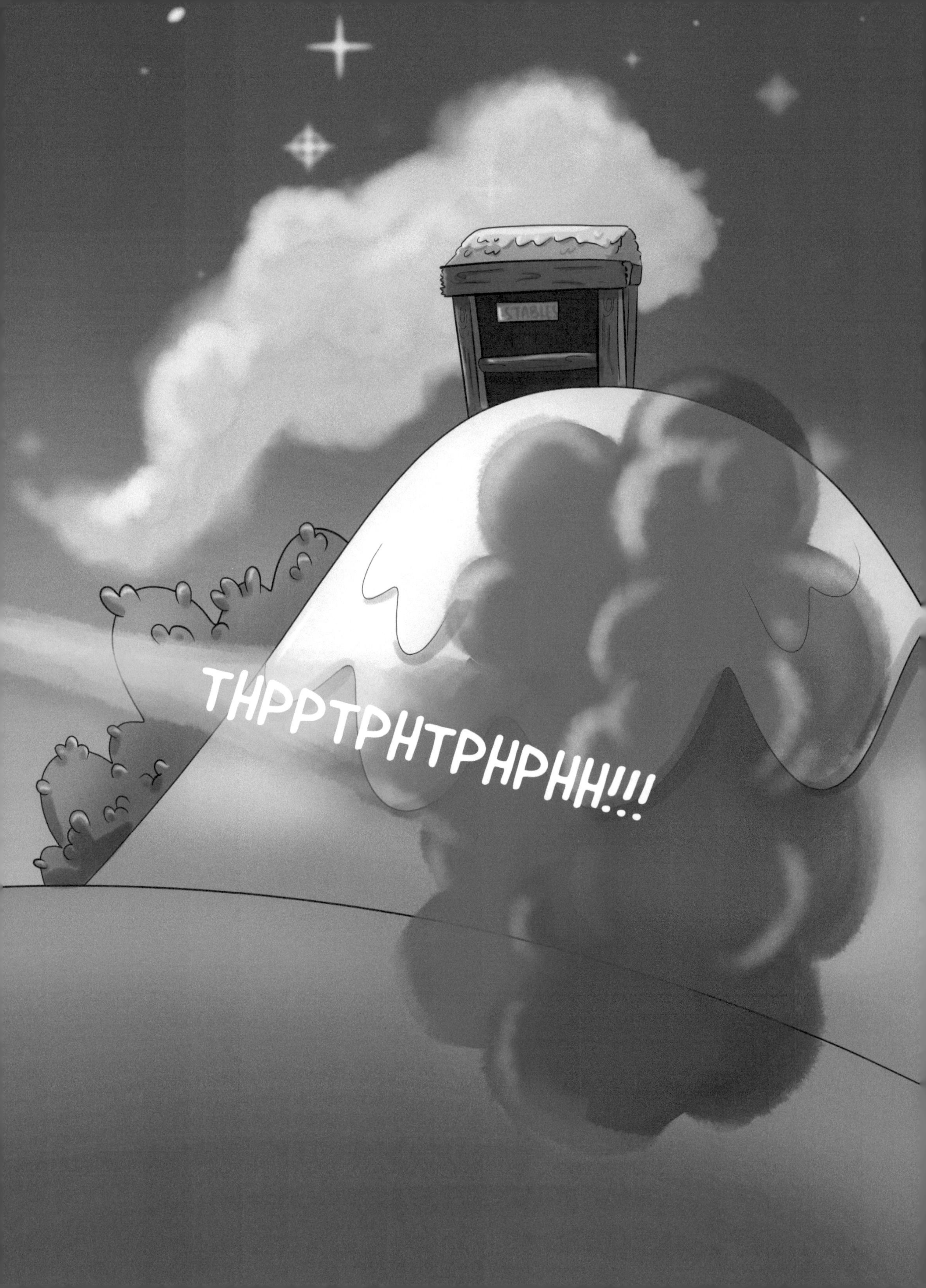
THPPTPHTPHPHH!!!

With Santa's team so old and slow,
they needed something with more gusto.

WHOOOOPFF

I suggested Remmy to be on the team,
as he would make their squad supreme.

It took Santa time to agree with me,
but it made Remmy shout a big WHOOPEE!!!
With a bowl of ice cream in front of his face,
he helped Santa's sleigh to get back on pace!

Now we need your help! If you'd be so sweet,
leave a bowl of ice cream for Remmy to eat.
We won't make it through the whole Christmas Eve,
if you don't help us out and truly believe.

Still leave the cookies and milk for St. Nick,
but now also ice cream to do the trick.

If you hear an explosion
and see a rainbow.
You don't need to worry
it's just Remmy oh!

POOOOOPFFGH

But what if your friends don't know about Remmy?
We need you to go and tell your ol' Gremmy...
I mean Grammy... and your friend named Sammy...
or those named Hammy... Wammy Kablammy.

Now thanks to you, Remmy won't be a zero,
as you'll help him out in becoming a hero!

fweet

I now undestand why it is so vital, for Remmy's ol' name to be in the title.

CPSIA information can be obtained
at www.ICGtesting.com
Printed in the USA
LVHW021938281019
635541LV00003B/364/P